When Stephanie Smiled . . .

story by Jeanne Willis
with pictures by Penelope Jossen

Andersen Press
London

Text copyright © 2003 by Jeanne Willis.
Illustrations copyright © 2003 by Penelope Jossen.
The rights of Jeanne Willis and Penelope Jossen to be identified as the author and illustrator
of this work have been asserted by them in accordance with the Copyright, Designs and Patents Act, 1988.

First published in Great Britain in 2003 by Andersen Press Ltd., 20 Vauxhall Bridge Road, London SW1V 2SA.
Published in Australia by Random House Australia Pty., 20 Alfred Street, Milsons Point, Sydney, NSW 2061.
All rights reserved. Colour separated in Italy by Fotoriproduzioni Grafiche, Verona.
Printed and bound in Italy by Grafiche AZ, Verona.

10   9   8   7   6   5   4   3   2   1

British Library Cataloguing in Publication Data available.

ISBN 1 84270 075 8

This book has been printed on acid-free paper

It was Monday. It was raining. It was maths.
James wasn't happy.
He wished it was Saturday and sunny and that
eleven take seven was five.
But it wasn't.

Then in walked Stephanie.

"Sit next to James," said the teacher.

Stephanie smiled.
Suddenly for James, magical things
started to happen . . .

The rain clouds turned
into dolphins . . .

. . . looping-the-loop in the sky.

Eleven take seven was four!
Monday was the best day of the week!
And all because Stephanie smiled.
They held hands under the desk . . .

Suddenly the teacher turned into a wise and beautiful queen.
The boy at the back who liked to pinch and punch
was nothing but a timid little mouse.

James had never felt happier.

"Life is wonderful!" he shouted.
Stephanie smiled.
He felt like a king in a scarlet cloak.
On his head was a golden crown.
His pen was a mighty sword.

Stephanie smiled at him over her skipping rope.

They smiled at each other during Country Dance.

They got married in the school play and everybody smiled.

James was so happy, he couldn't
wait to go to school.
Every single day was full of smiles.

But then, at the end of summer . . .

. . . Stephanie told him she was leaving.
She was going to live in another country,
thousands of miles away.
Goodbye, James.

He frowned.
His smile had gone.
Suddenly for James, terrible things
started to happen . . .

The rain clouds turned into sharks.

The teacher turned into a witch.

The boy at the back turned into a monkey
and stole his golden crown.
James went home . . .

He threw himself onto his bed.
"Life is horrid!" he cried.
He curled up with his face against the wall.
"Give us a smile," said his Dad.

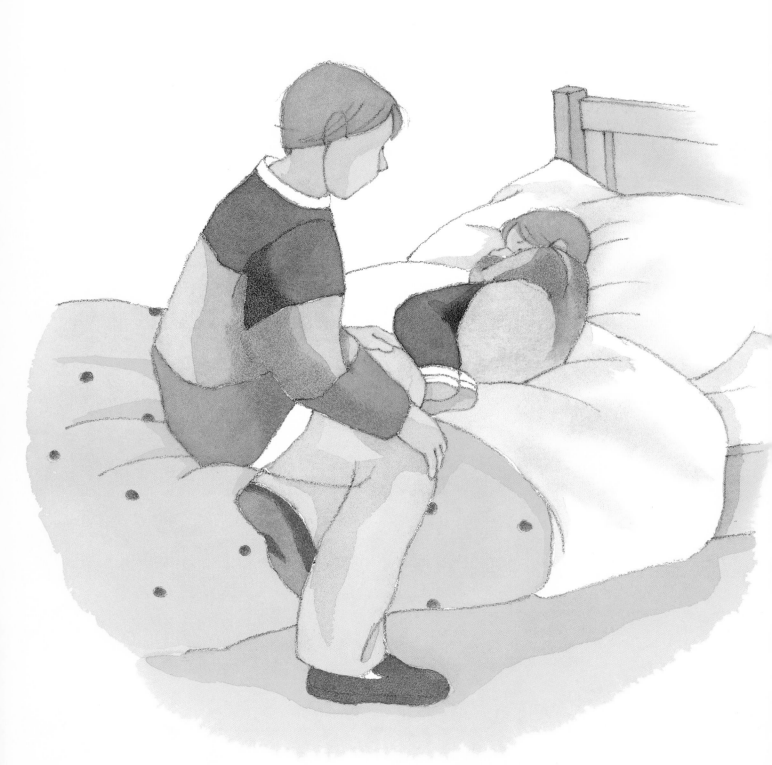

"I can't," said James. "Stephanie took it.
My smile has gone forever."
"It'll come back," said his mum, "I promise."

And she was right.

On Wednesday, in walked Wendy.

She sat next to James . . .
and gave him the biggest smile he'd ever seen.

for
Léa and Chelsea with
much love – P.J